SIHA TOOSKIN KNOWS

The Love of the Dance

By Charlene Bearhead and Wilson Bearhead
Illustrated by Chloe Bluebird Mustooch

HIGHWATER PRESS

Canada Council   Conseil des arts
for the Arts   du Canada

We acknowledge the support of the Canada Council for the Arts.
Nous remercions le Conseil des arts du Canada de son soutien.

HighWater Press gratefully acknowledges the financial support of the Province of Manitoba through the Department of Sport, Culture and Heritage and the Manitoba Book Publishing Tax Credit, and the Government of Canada through the Canada Book Fund (CBF), for our publishing activities.

HighWater Press is an imprint of Portage & Main Press.
Printed and bound in Canada by Friesens
Design by Relish New Brand Experience
Cover Art by Chloe Bluebird Mustooch

Library and Archives Canada Cataloguing in Publication

Title: Siha Tooskin knows the love of the dance / by Charlene Bearhead and
   Wilson Bearhead ; illustrated by Chloe Bluebird Mustooch.
Other titles: Love of the dance
Names: Bearhead, Charlene, 1963- author. | Bearhead, Wilson, 1958- author. |
Mustooch, Chloe Bluebird, 1991- illustrator.
Identifiers: Canadiana (print) 20190046953 | Canadiana (ebook) 20190047437
| ISBN 9781553798521 (softcover) | ISBN 9781553798545 (PDF) | ISBN
9781553798538 (iPad fixed layout)
Classification: LCC PS8603.E245 S54 2020 | DDC jC813/.6—dc23

23 22 21 20   1 2 3 4 5

HIGHWATER
PRESS
www.highwaterpress.com
Winnipeg, Manitoba
Treaty 1 Territory and homeland of the Métis Nation

people had great respect for the eagle staff, the regalia, the drums, the songs, and the dances. Jeff could see how proud the people were and he felt so proud and honoured to be part of the celebration as he watched his friend dance into the arbour.

After the prayers and the opening protocols were finished Jeff dropped into his chair. He didn't know if he was sweating more because of the hot weather or his anxiety about doing the wrong thing. All he knew was that he wished he had an eagle fan like Paul and Uncle Lenard to cool himself off with. Or maybe he should have slipped a little electric fan into his bag. People might have laughed at him, but it would feel so good right now.

Jeff watched the dancers and all of their different styles of dancing. In the beginning, Jeff couldn't keep his eyes off of Paul and Uncle Lenard. He saw his friend in a way that he never had before, and it was amazing.

As the powerful beat of the drum and the strong voices of the singers continued to fill the air, Jeff's eyes wandered from dancer to dancer. He marvelled at the beauty of the regalia and the uniqueness of each dancer's style.

Before he even noticed that they were gone from the arbour Paul and Uncle Lenard were sitting in their chairs beside Jeff. "It's a warm evening and I'm getting old," Uncle Lenard laughed. "Only three intertribals and I already need a rest and some water from the cooler."

Jeff laughed and pulled a bottle of water out of the cooler for Uncle Lenard. "Does everyone keep dancing like this all night?" He asked his question as he passed Paul a bottle of water. "I'm not even that old and I wouldn't be able to last that long. Dancing at a powwow takes a lot of energy."

"Not every dancer dances every song," Uncle Lenard answered, after taking a long drink of water. "These are called *intertribals*. All of the dancers dance together on these ones. Even other people who are not dressed in their regalia can dance in intertribals. There are always a few intertribals right after each Grand Entry and then from time to time during the powwow."

Now it made sense to Jeff. He had heard the announcer calling, "Intertribal—everybody dance," but he didn't know what an intertribal was. He also wondered why there were some people dressed in their regular clothes out dancing in the arbour. Even some non-Indigenous guests were dancing.

"Yup," added Paul. "Pretty soon they are going to start with the categories. When they do that all of the dancers have to clear the arbour and only the category that the announcer calls can be there. When they call 'junior boys Grass' that's my turn. I'll dance with other boys my age who are Grass dancers. Then I can also dance in the intertribals between categories when they have them."

Jeff nodded his head to show Paul that he was following what Paul was telling him. He remembered the first time that Paul had shown Jeff his regalia. Paul had explained that he was a Grass dancer and that was why he had long strands of coloured wool hanging from his shirt, leggings, and breechcloths. Paul had explained that when he danced he would weave and sway back and forth like the long prairie grass in the wind. Paul had explained to Jeff that long ago the Grass dancers would go ahead of the people when it was time to move and set up a new camp or lodge. These men would dance this way, weaving and swaying and stamping their feet to flatten down the long grass, until it formed a thick, soft pad on the ground that they could set up their tipis and lodges on.

"You're not a Grass dancer, right?" Jeff asked Uncle Lenard. "I don't see any wool or long ribbons on your regalia."

"Good eye," answered Uncle Lenard after another swig of water. "I dance men's Traditional."

"So what's that?" Jeff asked with great interest.

"Men's traditional dancers can be warriors or hunters. Some dances tell stories about tracking enemies or animals in a hunt. That dance is called

a Sneak-Up. There are also what we call straight traditional dances where men dance their own style as warriors or hunters."

"There's also men's Fancy Bustle," chimed in Paul. "That one is so awesome. The men are really fast and athletic. They are really bright and colourful and they spin and pivot and some even do cartwheels!!!"

"Wow," responded Jeff in amazement. He knew what a bustle was because he had watched Paul's dad working on a bustle for one of his nephews. Jeff remembered being in awe of how intricate the work was as Paul's dad had carefully placed each feather and tacked it in place. It all seemed so delicate, and he couldn't believe that a dancer could do all of that with a bustle tied to his back. Jeff was even more impressed when Paul told him that the men's Fancy dancers wore two bustles!

Uncle Lenard explained, "The men's Fancy Dance actually comes from Oklahoma, but men all over Turtle Island have adopted the dance."

"Sure, I saw them in the Grand Entry," Jeff responded with a bright smile and a sparkle in his eye. "I can't wait to see them dance in their category. It sounds awesome."

"My cousin Bobby might be here and he dances men's Fancy now, I think," Paul told Jeff.

"No, he's Chicken," corrected Uncle Lenard.

"Awww, that's sad," sympathized Jeff. "Is it the loud sound of the drum that scares him or is he just too shy to dance?"

Paul and Uncle Lenard laughed heartily. "He's not scared," Uncle Lenard clarified. "Men's Chicken dancers dance an old style that represents the motions and actions of the prairie chicken. I've been told that it comes from Southern Alberta in Blackfoot country originally."

"Oh," laughed Jeff with some embarrassment. "I wondered why someone would be scared of this. The Chicken dancer might have asked me the same thing, if he saw how much I was sweating when I first got here. I really didn't know what to expect, but this is awesome."

Paul smiled at his friend, reassuring him. "My mom loves watching the Chicken dancers. They are her favourite. She says that she especially loves watching the little ones as they strut around and imitate the head motions of the prairie chicken."

"Uncle, look," Paul called out excitedly. "There's Leanne. I didn't know they were coming this weekend." Paul and his uncle looked over at the young women preparing to dance in the teen girls' Fancy category. Jeff wasn't sure who they were talking about, but Paul waved and a young woman with a yellow shawl smiled and nodded back at him as she prepared to dance in her category.

"That's my cousin Leanne," Paul explained to Jeff. "She lives in Saskatchewan with her family but sometimes they come out here to dance. I thought they were going to be at a different powwow in Saskatchewan but I'm glad that we get to see them. She's really good. Watch her."

"Cool," replied Jeff. "What kind of dance is this?"

"It's teen girls' Fancy Shawl," replied Paul. "We usually just call it ladies' Fancy."

"Do they try to outdo each other like in the men's Fancy?" Jeff asked with increased curiosity.

"Ladies' Fancy is different," Uncle Lenard began to explain.

"Some people say that the Shawl dancers imitate a butterfly. The story that I was told is that the ladies' Fancy Dance is about a woman who was in mourning after the death of her husband. It was said that after she mourned for one year she was ready to come back to the circle. The dance is her way of showing that she is alive and ready to express her joy for life like a beautiful butterfly after it comes out of a cocoon."

"They really do look beautiful," said Paul. He watched the young women spin and kick up their feet as their arms moved swiftly and gracefully, making their shawls flow around them.

"And their outfits are really colourful and beautiful like butterflies, too," added Jeff.

Uncle Lenard had been listening to the boys as he checked out his own bustle to ensure that no feathers had come loose before it was his turn to dance again. "They are really beautiful. The regalia is beautiful, but the spirit of our dances and our ways are the real strength and beauty. It's hard to believe that the colonial governments that came to our lands thought it would be a good idea to make this illegal, isn't it?"

"What do you mean by 'make this illegal'?" asked Jeff, looking totally confused. He had learned from Ms. Baxter that the British government and then Canada had forced many laws on First Nations people on their own land, but he had not heard anything about the powwow being against the law.

"Yup, just like the potlatch of our brothers and sisters to the west and so many of the ceremonies of the other Nations that lived on these lands long before settlers, the governments imposed laws on our people making it illegal for us to gather and to dance powwow."

Paul looked very sad just thinking about it, while Jeff just looked shocked. "I don't get it," Jeff wondered aloud. "How could something as beautiful and positive and fun as a powwow be against the law?"

"I'm so glad that our people are so strong," Paul asserted with a proud smile. "I can't even imagine not being able to express myself and who I am this way…and I sure can't imagine not being able to hang out with my cousins and my other relatives."

"I can't imagine you not being able to have a bannock burger every weekend," chuckled Uncle Lenard. "It was the courage and faith of our people that kept our ways alive, but it was also our humour that carried us through. So who wants a bannock burger? I'm going for the bannock taco personally."

"When will they dance again?" asked Jeff after the category had finished and the girls were walking to line up at the front of the arbour.

"Wow, you didn't get that excited when I finished dancing. Settle down—I know they are beautiful, but they are my cousins too, bro," teased Paul. "They might have some intertribals between the ladies' categories or they might finish up all of the junior ladies' categories first. Don't worry, they aren't going anywhere."

Jeff blushed and he could feel the sweat coming back to his forehead, but this time he knew it was because he was embarrassed. He gave Paul a little nudge and then was happy to hear the clink, clink, clink of small metal cones as the junior ladies Jingle Dress dancers were called to the dancing area by the announcer.

"I guess they are going to finish all of the junior ladies right away," explained Paul, as he watched the girls find their own spaces in the arbour and get themselves into their starting positions.

"The one in the purple and white is Lisa, Leanne's sister," Paul exclaimed as he excitedly pointed out his cousin to Jeff. "She dances Jingle like her mom."

"I like the sound of those little bells," Jeff said as he watched the dancers intently. He quickly caught himself and added, "The same way I like the sound of the deer hooves clicking together on your ankles."

"Lisa's bells are called *jingles*," Paul explained, grinning at Jeff. "This dance is special to our relatives because it's an Ojibway medicine dance and some of my mom's relatives are Ojibway. Now lots of women from all different Nations dance Jingle. My baby sister Laura will be a Jingle dancer, I hope." Paul paused, looking thoughtful. "When my Mugoshin Mary, my mom's auntie, was young she was given the right to dance Jingle. She told me that back in the day you only danced Jingle if you had been given the right. That's because it's a medicine dance. My mom says that times change and we change with them, so now many women and girls

dance Jingle because they choose that style of dance for powwow."

"What is a medicine dance?" asked Jeff. "Does it make people better?"

"Some people still know the story of how this healing dance was given many years ago," answered Uncle Lenard. "Many years ago an Ojibway woman had a dream..." He continued.

"Her people were living in a time of great sickness, and she had a dream that would help them get better. It is said that in her dream she was given a dress to make. The dress had 365 shells on it to represent each day of the year. She also saw in the dream that the dancers should dance sideways as they shuffle their feet. In that way they would make the shells clink together to get the attention of the Creator: the dance is the prayer."

"The dance has changed a lot over the years," recalled Uncle Lenard. "Now many of the girls dance faster, almost like Fancy dancers. We still see the old style though. Now they call it the Ojibway Round Dance or a Side Step. Maybe they'll do one of these songs this weekend and you'll see what I mean. If they do, I'll show you the difference."

Jeff was listening closely although he still looked a bit confused. "Those things don't look like shells," he said to Uncle Lenard.

"You're right," Uncle Lenard replied. "That has changed too. Now the dresses have metal cones called jingles instead. You know...modern." He laughed.

Jeff watched as the girls gracefully wove their way in and out, in a winding pattern around the arbour. He thought that this might be his favourite category of dancing because he really liked the sound of the jingles and he loved the story of this very meaningful dance.

After the Jingle Dress dancers had finished, they cleared the dance area. Jeff heard the announcer call out, "All junior ladies Traditional dancers come to the centre of the circle. Ladies Traditional, get ready. You're up next."

Jeff turned his head sharply towards Uncle Lenard. "The ladies don't dance like they are tracking enemies and hunting animals, do they?"

"No," laughed Uncle Lenard as he watched the look of relief settle on Jeff's face. "They're called ladies Traditional because this is the original women's style of dancing that really came from the old times. Long ago, women didn't dance in the arbour like the men do. They would dance in one spot as they stood in a circle behind the men who sang at the drum, and they would help with the singing. Later, as powwow changed, the women's Traditional became a category of dance all its own."

"Oh I see," replied Jeff thoughtfully. He looked out over the women dancing in the arbour. His eyes moved from dancer to dancer, then to the drummers who sang the powerful songs and then on to all of the other dancers standing in their regalia as they watched the categories. Jeff was overwhelmed by the beauty of the dancers in their regalia, the strength in the drum and the voices of the singers, and by the incredible feeling of belonging that everyone seemed to have in the circle. Jeff was mostly amazed at how peaceful he felt in that circle.

"Well, ishawin," Paul nudged his uncle. "How about we go dance a couple of intertribals now?"

"Sounds good, Siha Tooskin." Uncle Lenard then turned to Jeff and added, "Are you coming too, Eeshta ta?"

"What does that mean?" Jeff asked with great curiosity.

"It means the one with the big eyes," Uncle Lenard laughed. "It's good the way you open your eyes to take this all in. That's how you learn. That's going to be my name for you. So do you want to join us for an intertribal or are you going to stay here with your big eyes opened wide to take in even more?"

Jeff laughed. He liked his new name. He didn't know what made him happier: the fact that Uncle Lenard had given him his own name or that Uncle Lenard was now joking with him the same way he joked with Paul. "I think I'll stay here and use my 'eeshta ta' for a while until I get this right. Then I'll come and try my moves a little later."

Uncle Lenard and Paul laughed as they moved towards the dance area. They knew that it wouldn't be long before Jeff would be out there with them dancing his own style in an intertribal.